Razzamadaddy

by Linda Walvoord
illustrated by Sachiko Yoshikawa

MARSHALL CAVENDISH
NEW YORK · LONDON · SINGAPORE

Marshall Cavendish, 99 White Plains Road, Tarrytown, NY 10591
www.marshallcavendish.com

Library of Congress Cataloging-in-Publication Data
Walvoord, Linda.
Razzamadaddy / by Linda Walvoord ; illustrations by Sachiko Yoshikawa.— 1st ed.
p. cm.
Summary: A father and son spend a wonderful day together at the beach.
ISBN 0-7614-5158-7
[1. Fathers and sons—Fiction. 2. Beaches—Fiction. 3. Stories in
rhyme.] I. Yoshikawa, Sachiko, ill. II. Title.
PZS.3.W1993Raz 2004
[E]—dc21
2003009319

The text of this book is set in 15-point Barbera.
The illustrations are rendered in acrylic and pastel on watercolor paper.
Printed in China
First edition
2 4 6 5 3 1

One Daddy, two Daddy,
Three Daddy, four.
Come, Daddy, go Daddy,
Open the door!

Laundry

Up Daddy, out Daddy,
Zoom Daddy, me.
Down Daddy, town Daddy,
Fiddle-dee-dee!

Hey Daddy, haw Daddy,
Foot to the floor.
Me next to Daddy,
Rumble and roar.

Zip doodle, trip doodle,
Daddy and me.
Fiddle dum, diddle dum,
Down to the sea.

Beach

Piggyback, zig Daddy,
Giddyap, jig.
Pitching me, ditching me,
Zag and a zig.

Race me and chase me,
I'll run away!
Tackle me, tickle me,
Ho Daddy, hey.

Pitter kick, patter kick,
Flutter my toes.
I can dip under, Dad,
Holding my nose.

Bubble me, puddle me,
Feet off the ground.

Paddle and kick, Daddy,

Don't let me down.

Shovel and pail, Daddy,
Let's make a wall.
A tower, a sand castle,
Rounded and tall.

Pack higher, pat higher,
Squeezing my hand.
Dribble a tower,
Ripple the sand.

Fee-fi-fo-fum, Daddy,
I'll be the knight.
You be the dragon,
Let's have a fight!

Over the parapet,
Dragon is rumbling,
Slosh buckle, swashbuckle,
Dragon is tumbling.

Under the sand, Daddy,
You disappear.
Wiggle me, giggle me,
Now you're all here.

Hot dog, potato chips,
Mustard and pop.
Splat goes the ketchup,
Slippity slop.

Ice cream for us, Daddy,
Whistle and whoop.
I'd like some chocolate,
Dribbly scoop.

Roll the ball, catch the ball,
Where did it go?
Dilly ball, silly ball,
Up high, down low.

Throw the ball harder, whee!
Daddy, go catch.
Here's a humdinger,
Daddy, now watch!

Somebody's mellowing
Trumpety tunes.
Razzamadaddy
Over the dunes.

Whirl, Daddy, twirl, Daddy,
Swing me some more.

Fishing boats bobbing
Far from the shore.

Seagulls are sweeping by
Almost in reach.
Picker up, litter up,
Cleaning the beach.

Pearly pale seashells
Sit in my hands.
Shimmery, glimmery,
Plucked from the sand.

Dance me now, prance me now,
Swing me up high.
Blues, Daddy, horn, Daddy,
Milky Way sky.

Patty-cake, Daddy cake,
Where did we roam?

Clappy me, happy me,
All the way home.